Published by Ad Hoc Fiction.
www.AdHocFiction.com

Purchasing Information:
Paperback available from www.AdHocFiction.com
E-book available from all usual outlets.

Printed Worldwide.
First Printing 2020.

ISBN paperback 978-1-912095-50-6
ISBN e-Book 978-1-912095-49-0

Don't Tell the Bees

by

Mary-Jane Holmes

AdHoc Fiction

Forward and back,
Went drearily singing the chore-girl small,
Draping each hive with a shred of black.

JOHN GREENLEAF WHITTIER

Contents

Postpartum

She'd mottled like a gull's egg in the carrying of her, left the bairn newly birthed, howling in twitch grass by the river; returned to her wheel to draft wool skeins, skirts crusted brown, foot against the treadle, fast and even.

Her husband found it, batted the flies from the cord freshly cut, took the bawling child in his great flat palms and the babby calmed, took to suckling his knuckle still sweet with wood sap.

He pressed his wife to take the infant back, held her raw hands, once as smooth as corn-silk; called her *harvest moon* as he'd done summers ago in the stubble of the twelve-acre. But with each appeal, she plucked a sheaf of her hair and taking up her spindle, twisted the shafts to a silver ply that coiled like steel around her.

The child whined, beat the lattice of his ribs for love or hunger so he fossicked a horse bridle to hold her and that was how he worked – daughter hoyed across his back in quarry and field until spring, when driving his pony string from shoreline to pithead he unhitched the girl, for the bridle was needed for the journey; left her at her mother's feet playing with the rovings that fell from her spinner, hoping her laughter might feather his wife's heart.

When he returned, a hundred gold sovereigns lighting his wallet, a wattled crib swinging from his side, he found the farm deserted but tied from the spinning wheel - a noil of thread which he followed past alder groves and drying sheds to the banks of the river. There was his daughter at the water's edge: naked, cough-kinked. He scooped her up, swaddled her as best he could but nothing, not even his knuckle dipped in bee-bread stemmed the crying.

Then he saw it: a shimmer of cloth caught in shingle on the bank. He unhooked it. So soft. Delicate as shell. Held to his cheek, he heard it sigh something akin to the crepitation of hay, felt its weft of eye and limb upon him as he wrapped the child within it and lay her cooing in the crib.

Rumour

No-one could remember her real name, but throughout the marshlands from Damvix to Gruelle, everyone knew the story of little *No-more* Picard from Mazanou, how her mother, Katrine, rejected her, left her for dead and as for the name, there were those that heard it was the words, *no more*, in rhythm with the spin of the wheel, the mother muttered over and over again. This was how it was told up and down the marts and washhouses of the flatlands. When Constantine her oldest son and his brothers, bar Felix, the youngest, who was only past toddling, left the village soon after, this was added to the story too. The men, sleeves rolled past their elbows, slapped cattle onto trailer pens lamenting the draw of the cities that took the best brawn from the land, while the women admonished so harshly this mother, who'd abandoned one of her own and drove out the remaining, that they ran their skin raw against the zinc of their washboards feeling the sting of lye soap for weeks after.

The Surveyor

The morning before the storm, a man arrived in Mazanou driving an automobile and wearing twill britches. He set about the village holding a little wheel attached to a long handle. The wheel clicked as it turned and the man stopped from time to time, at a curve in the road or a crossroads and scribbled on a piece of paper he carried in the buttonhole pocket of his matching twill jacket. The villagers, certain that no good could come from such scrutiny, slid out through back doors to blanket copper stills and closet unlicensed shotguns, so when the man called through open windows and un-shuttered front doors to ask if anyone was home, the only answer was the hollow swing of beaded fly screens.

The silence unnerved the man. He had passed through all the villages in the marshlands and had found them to be lively, bustling little places, each with a café with Battenberg lace pinned across the window and a port where green-painted punts bobbed cheerfully in the water. Yet in Mazanou, he found only buckled cart axles in the main square and the few row boats apparent lay bottom-up and bleached on the canal bank.

In front of the church, beside its modest fountain, he stopped. Even the water, a thin ferrous trickle seeping from a lead spigot, seemed as reluctant as the inhabitants to admit its presence. He sat at its edge, sending salamanders scuttling under a stack of washing dollies and slipped off a shoe to confirm the blister he'd felt bubble where the sock yarn had rubbed thin on his heel. He searched for his handkerchief to cushion the swelling, pulling out his pocket watch and noting the time as he did so. He looked up into the skirts of the two great bells that hung in the tower above him only to find their tongues lashed to the strike.

He wondered which saint the church was dedicated to but found no inscription or bulletin for Matins or Sunday service. It struck him that there were no signposts in Mazanou, or house numbers, no street names posted, no enamel plaques marking a *Place de la Revolution* or *La Route de Paris*. There was in fact nothing or no-one to say the place existed at all.

It was then he heard the tut-tutting slap of footsteps running across cobbles. They stopped in the shadows the spire was poking accusingly along the rutted corners of the square and the man rose, hands visored to see who might be there. A child, barefoot, her hands clasped to her chest as if in prayer stood as motionless as her surroundings.

'Look' she said, her eyes as wide as pocket mirrors and the man leaned in, watching her unhinge her cupped fingers. A damselfly pulsated on her palm, its wings papery and long veined, its abdomen rising and falling as if filled with breath. 'They sew up your eyes and mouth if you say something bad,' she said, fluttering her fingers and they watched it lift and zig-zag about them.

While the man strained to track the insect's dart, he felt a tug at his cuffs. The girl was staring at the little trundle wheel he'd left leant against the fountain.

'It's for measuring,' he said, showing her how each revolution marked a certain distance as he rolled it along the ground. The wheel tick-ticked across the stones and she clapped her hands against her thighs, mouthing the increments of distance, nodding, nodding, yes, yes she said, her feet hot-footing, her hands stretched for the handle and when he gave it to her she sprang round and bolted down a thin ginnel before appearing up another laughing '10 rods to the ash closets, 5 chains to the forge, an arpent to the tannery!'

The man laughed, noting her distances, measurements he had already recorded, and was surprised at the swiftness and exactitude from a child who couldn't be older than twelve. He asked her what she was called and she replied *No-more.* He laughed and said that was the strangest name he had ever heard, then he asked her if the streets had names and she rattled off such a strange litany, Cat Nest Ghaut, Squeeze Gut Alley, Arguments Yard, that he began to doubt the girl was all there but when they came to a lane where the houses and byres petered out, the girl looked past the scratchy poplars that lined the track and said it wasn't called anything and didn't lead anywhere so they turned and doubled backed the way they had come, the girl only taking up her counting again once they were passed the sentry of trees.

The villagers unfolded their shadows from doorways and watched the pair walk the poplar track as far as Hang Lane and turn back again, the Picard girl skipping the wheel along the blackthorn, the man walking alongside, pen pointing at the sky, a handkerchief flapping from his shoe like a little red flag.

No-more

No-more loved to count. As a baby, strapped to her father's back, she counted the strike of the mattock and the swing of the scythe, feeling her father's lattice of ribs against her own, marking the space between each pulse of his heart. These were her first memories. When she could walk she counted the things that ran from her – the parading geese, their fattening livers slung low in their bellies, the moley-rats that mined the corn store, the days her mother, face flinted, stayed indoors behind closed shutters. Later, she followed her brother Felix to school, swinging her satchel along the canal tow path. She knew how many alder trees lined the banks, how many tobacco kilns studded the fields, the exact number of footsteps to the playground gates. There she watched the other children skip elastic and throw Jacks and she longed to join them but the others didn't like the way she muttered numbers under her breath, so they kept her away.

One day, the spark of a storm in the air, No-more was counting ants emptying their colony of larvae by the perimeter fence of the school, when Pascal Sylvain who sat in front of her in class and whose hair was as smooth as elvers, came and crouched beside her.

'Look they're moving house,' said No-more making room for her new playmate. 'The weather must be changing.'

Pascal poked the nest with a stick and they watched the insects swell about it. Then he asked No-more to pull up her pinafore and when she wouldn't, he pushed her into the grass where the ants swarmed her legs and undergarments and he ran back to the others who were playing catch-a-frog on the school steps.

Nomore ran to her brother who was never in school but always playing craps with the older boys by the canal, cheroots tucked behind their ears, pocketknives in leather pouches clipped to their belts. She showed him the bites blazing her skin. She told him about the stick and what Pascal did and Felix listened, the dice bouncing in his palm and then he threw a double six. 'Count yourself lucky,' he laughed, but she didn't know how to begin.

Felix

After school, Felix stole a car and drove it past the abattoir to show the lads he was going places. He'd found it at the edge of Mr Sylvain's angelica field, keys glinting on the dashboard. There were women just over the hedge, stripping leaves and stems for the bitters to be sent to Paris as a cure for over-indulgence. He heard them laughing and shushing the infants left on the shady canal banks as he pulled the chrome handle and climbed in. This was not the first thing he had stolen. When his father sent him to scarecrow Mr Sylvain's beet field, he loped off instead to pick vine squash in the neighbouring plot, to see if Madam Bazin would shoot the old Chassepot rifle she kept loaded by her front porch.

The bullet kicked the fruit from his hands, sprayed his shirt with thick orange flesh, the pips stuck to his collarbones. Later that season when the swamp-gnat made the old girl's spleen swell ripe with chills, he stole that gun, slipped it between the spindles in the well-shaft, charged fivepence to any boy who didn't believe he'd done it, letting them pull it from its ferned hidey-hole to look down its sights.

This car, with its curved running boards and double-chevron grill, looked just the type to be filled with an arsenal of firearms, like the one he'd seen when the travelling picture house set up its screen in Rigal's twelve-acre; full of men with sharp suits and girls called 'doll' or 'sweet-pea' driving along broad boulevards, devoid of horse shit or potholes. When he slid in behind the wheel, he opened the glove box, hoping for a small revolver, a bundle of cash, but there was only a cotton scroll full of tools he didn't know the names of and a magazine with the picture of a girl with a marguerite pinned behind one ear. Her eyes followed him as he lifted the cover to the windscreen for a better look. The light filled out the girl's smile. He folded back the paper, tore out her face and slipped it into his breast pocket where he kept his card-game winnings and when he sounded the horn at the boys pulling carcasses on to drays, and they looked up, wiping the blood off their aprons with their knuckles, he pressed down hard on the accelerator knowing he could do anything, go anywhere, wondering where his sweet pea might live and if he might steal her heart.

The Weathervane

Maurice Picard rattled the fixings of the thin metal ladder that ran the height of the spire and adjusted his tool belt. Below him, Gerard Rigal's goats coursed the graveyard, strewing chrysanthemum petals across the airy mounds of freshly piled earth. Above him, the weathervane listed eastwards, the flashing from under it split and curled, its cockerel lurching as if readying for flight. Maurice climbed towards it. The wind was sharp at his back, and his hollow tooth throbbed, the remnants of the storm still gusting in its root. His teeth were better than any wall-hung barometer. He'd felt the weather coming the day before as he set a new lintel across the gable end of Pappy Parnell's milking parlour, glad of the work and the mild October temperatures to get the task done. Late swallows threaded the telegraph pole as he measured the stone, driving the plugs and shims through the split line. It was then his molars started humming, like the quiet vibration on a train rail. He blamed it on the fall of the hammer, but by evening his jaw raged premonition and the birds had flown.

That night, a bull's eye squall bubbled off the Atlantic and charged the coast. In Fontenay, it flattened the perimeter of the small zoo and there was talk of caimans slipping into the canals, but in Mazanou only the church was struck. Maurice was not a superstitious man and paid no mind to those who talked of omens; he'd volunteered to repair the damage because he'd watched his father, when the century was still fresh, hammer and bellow life into the finials and wind cups of the mechanism, helping him scratch his initials on the glowing tail feathers of the bird freshly forged. Of this he was proud, and he didn't like to see his family honour skewed off its fixings.

But now the whole thing looked crude and comical, this squat bird with its chamfered eye and comb smeared white with guano, and he took the scutch from his belt to scrape it clean, but the pain rose again and sang across the fissured enamel of his teeth. He looked towards the west wondering if another front was forming, but there was nothing but the furzy haze lifting off the marshland and sunlight glinting off truck sidings on the ocean road. At this height he could see the future, the outline of rising cities, the criss-cross of new tarmacadam—a world he'd lost his sons to, a world a man like him, *an artisan*, could surely thrive in, be valued even and be done with splitting stone for centimes. Yes, that was what he must do.

The cockerel quivered in the briny air, and he grabbed its shaft with both hands. It bent easily back into shape, and he worked a fresh apron of flashing round its base, seaming it tight with his chase wedge. He lubricated the bearings and spindles just as the sun began to dip, and the bird shimmered in the low rays. He blinked through its brightness at the village heaped below him and traced the unpaved road to the glint of tin that was his own roof. In the yard, his youngest, his little girl, scattered grains, hens swarming at her feet. He waved and saw the child look up, her face a rosy moon against the rays of the sun. She set the feeder on her hip and lifted her arm to him then disappeared into the hen house to fetch the eggs. In the city, she will put her counting to use, he thought, feeling the evening breeze swell against his chest, hearing the newly greased cardinals swing. They revolved so freely and with such vigour that he felt the fall before it happened: the North point snagging on the collar of his overalls, the lift of his bowels as he dropped and the rush of comfort as the weight of his toothache dissolved into the surprisingly clement evening breeze.

Honey

No-more found six eggs in the hen house but they were all either pullet or wind eggs – small and yokeless. She didn't know why, perhaps the grain was poor or perhaps it was as old Madame Bazin said, an omen, a sign. She had so much to ask Papie, but his boots weren't yet by the door, instead she found her mother in the apiary smoking bees with a smudge stick of green tobacco leaves. The smoke wafted up through the hive as thick as marsh mist, making her mother's face look soft and dreamy around the edges like one of the picture-book princesses that lined the schoolroom, or the gauzy pin-ups Felix tacked to his bedroom wall. For a moment she forgot the burning on her legs and the prickle low against her groin when she thought of Pascal's fingers pulling at her hem, and instead she absorbed her mother scooping out the old brood combs, humming in tune to the buzzing edge of wings from the drowsy bees fanning her fingers. When her mother saw her, she smiled and offered her a brim of bee-bread from a dipper shaped like a wand and it tasted sweeter than anything she could have ever wished for.

Falling

Maurice Picard is falling. The ground beneath him is fine-grained and friable, newly spaded on the coffin of Jeannette Dubois, whose family, while the body cooled in the front parlour, turned each paving stone, each rotten floorboard for the fortune they knew she'd possessed and found nothing.

It is the same soil Maurice's mother gave birth to him on fifty years before, hunched over a scattering of straw on the kitchen's earthen floor, the same soil his father tilled until the pull of the horses tore at his sockets and buckled his back, the same soil stripped of hedgerow and coppice to allow Mr Sylvain's large tractors and combines through, the same soil Maurice sifts with lime to add a splash of warmth to a rendered wall and take the glare off it in the blistering midsummer. Its forgiving consistency and the fact that it has not had time to settle and compress over the remains of Mlle Dubois might perhaps be enough to save him.

It is, of course, a destiny he can only hope for as he is simply dropping through the air, the tools from his belt - his scutch and chase wedge and bird beak pliers - flying past his ears as he hurtles past pilaster, spandrel and quoin towards the loamy gleam of the graveyard. And all he can do is cushion his fall with hindsight and the good fortune of Jeanette Dubois which will spill a gold halo about him.

Wake

They buried Maurice four feet from where he fell. This was not lost on the men who wives told them *to stop that now* as they unwrapped cherry Clafoutie and handed round thimblefuls of Pineau de Charente liqueur. The men stood in half circles picking the eyes of potatoes from under their fingernails, far enough away from the pine coffin donated so generously by the Dubois family to not wonder at its size. It was said that after the fall he was as concertinaed as a squeeze box, his soft organs having fused to his heart, his neck lodged in his thorax.

Mr Sylvain set down his plate of untouched food and crossed the Picard's front parlour, to pay his respects to the widow, kissing her on both cheeks which made No-more hold her black shift tight across her knees. He nodded to his men who left their soupçons of wine on the buffet and clipped their braces back on their britches as they headed back out to the fields, leaving the women to wash and dry the chipped crockery and borrowed tumblers. When they too had gone, No-more found she was alone with only her dead father curled up in the box balanced on the undertaker's trestle table. It was not loss she felt exactly rather a sort of premonition like knowing the sum of two numbers without having to think and it was then she realized Mamie was not in the house, so she ran to the apiary where she found the hives upturned, the bees gone except the queen clinging to a brood-comb, abdomen heaving. Beside her Katrine, daubed in honey, was draping the hives with shreds of black. No-more took her by the hands, licking off the sweetness till there was no cry left in her mother. Then she fetched the goat shears from the gin-gang, cutting out the last strands of grief caught matted in her mother's hair.

A Girl's Guide to Frog Gigging

No-more dripped duckweed into the yard, a cowl of nutria round her neck strung up by their angry orange teeth. She'd pulled them from traps sunk along a stretch of marsh she had no right to be in, keeping her body low in the water so old Larnaudie, spit-polishing ball bearings by the landings, couldn't get a whiff of her and set to. Every so often, a frog mistook her skirt ballooning across the bubbling algae for a lily pad ,and she scooped it up, thudding its head against the alder roots that held the river bank and stuffing it into her knickers, for she knew that snaring water rat was one thing but there was no forgiveness for frog gigging these days.

'Give me that twine,' her mother said, taking the marlin spike from her mouth, setting it down on the halved cognac barrel serving as a makeshift work bench. No-more unhitched her brace of vermin, pulled the nylon cord out from under the limp bodies and handed it over. Her mother licked the ends and twisted the splice into the lengths of the skep she was working. It would be the fourth she'd made, the others swinging from the paltry coppice beside the pig huts and the bees yet to colonise any of them. No-more winced at the fervour of this fruitless industry when there was so much more to be done; how were they to pay Sylvain's rent? She was young but she sensed this was a type of craziness deeper veined than Thierry Begoux barking at the few automobiles that growled through the village, or Mathilde the seamstress sewing nightdresses for her kitty.

'Your brother can practise on those,' her mother said to No-more's catch, rearming her mouth with cow horn ready to de-pith and strop the bramble suckers for the binding. So, No-more gathered the wet shag of pelt by the tails and crossed the yard for the house, kicking at the tufty mole-hills sprouting in the lean spring sun. The warmth was welcome, the winter had been raw and with Mamie too dafty to oversee the planting, the brassicas and onion sets No-more had sowed had rooted shallow, only to curdle in the first hoarfrosts. They'd lived the latter end of the season on pickled cucumbers from the summer harvest, saving the softer conserves – the syrup- blanched persimmons and duck fritons – for Mamie who had stopped eating but No-more made her suck them through hollowed oat grass.

Felix was in the larder sharpening knives on the whetstone for his new job at the abattoir, his face churned pink with effort. When No-more picked up the pretty pearled handle of a tripe knife he snatched it from her and ran its serrated edge across the downy cut of her jaw. No-more did not move. She knew that to do so would only flame her brother's frustration that Mamie's old knives were past honing and that he had to work at the knackers yard. She listened to the dull blade scissor at her skin. Felix stopped when he saw the coypu and No-more bolted to the attic stairs shouting back that Mamie had said to flush them out good before hanging them.

In the attic, she lay on her mattress tracing the welts rising on her cheek. She thought of her other brothers, the ones she'd never known and wondered if they were as mean as Felix and that was why Papie and Mamie had never spoken of them.

She closed her eyes and wished there was someone to help her, wished her brothers home from the cities, knowing she would have to coop the chickens and pull Mamie from her canes and baskets before the dew fell and it was then something slipped warm against her abdomen. Reaching under her skirt she pulled out a frog. She held it up by its webby hands and it did not struggle, just hung there, its pale throat pumping. She kissed it, knowing for the first time the flush of hope madness brings. 'What a wise thing you are,' she said, and the frog blinked, eyes as glistery as shining armour.

Resistance

Mr Sylvain wakes, penis hard as a sculling oar. He gets up, stands at the window watching the moon sheening off Picard's dovecote. The dream he wakes from is always the same - the little white parachutes flutter through the juniper to land amongst the chanterelles, the silk rests soft against his collarbone as he cuts the ties tethering the squat packages, the money glinting through gummed brown paper. When he returns home, his mother sets down her apron, pours them a shot of her best cognac, listens to his plans, the land they will buy, the empire they will build, never questioning, never smiling only brushing her child's hair from out of his fevered eyes.

In the dream, he is never waist deep in the stink of butterbur, leeches a shudder against his calves. He does not feel the urine flush his thighs as he hears the slash of undergrowth a grass blade above him. In his dream, the two lads swinging Tilley lamps in the wake of the plane's growl, the oldest Picard, the oldest Larnaudie, whom he'd heard that morning in his mother's café downing their ersatz coffee of chicory and dandelion with a muted 'Vive la Liberté' are not found days later, hanged with the hollowed coins of Vichy filling their mouths.

Mr Sylvain returns to the warmth of his eiderdown. He wonders how Picard's widow will pay the rent this month and the overdue rent going back a year now since Maurice fell off the church. Looking out over the farm's cracked roof tiles, he feels the jump of blood lighten his groin.

Slaughter

Felix almost lost a hand in a shackling strap, herding hogs into the stick-pit. The gambrel hooks hanging from the rafters clinked as the other boys laughed. 'There, there, kid, could've been worse,' they said, rubbing their palms on their aprons. They had all been promoted to finer work – chuck-boners, tender-pullers, knuckle-droppers – except Felix who having just once snipped the entrails of one of Mr. Sylvain's prize-winning Gascon boars, the rumen spilling and tainting the meat, had forever been consigned to the killing floor.

He rubbed at the ligature mark the leather had left as the pigs fretted around him, hooves skittering on the sluiced quarry tiles. The veins on the back of his hands rose as the blood flushed back into his fingertips. He thought of his father's hands then, the same girth, the same stout fingers, nails rasped to the quick, but Maurice's had had calluses from making things: harling lime or working dressed stone, whereas Felix saw only the lacerations from cleavers and hatchet blades on his own.

A pig nuzzled at his thigh like a puppy or one of the ponies his father had bred for the mines – heavy limbed with plenty of bone and substance, willing temperaments – soft and intelligent. 'There, there,' said Felix, rubbing the rough bristle between its ears. 'There, there,' he said, feeling the wound pulsing across his palm, as he raised the pipe, as he closed his eyes.

Scarab

No-more shooed a pair of nesting magpies from out of one of the skeps. Trapped between the hive's binding she found a dead rose-chafer beetle. It shimmered in the burn of the sun like the eye of the peacock feather Mamie kept pinned to the vanity mirror in her bedroom, the plume Papie had found when he was replacing flagstones in the city. Mamie had thirty skeps swinging in the pollarded ash trees now, their bait combs withered, useless for attracting anything except wasps and vermin but there was no sign of her ceasing the coil, coil, coil of cane and willow, except each moon, when Mr. Sylvain came for the rent. Then Mamie left the wrapping-iron and bodkin aside and showed him into the house, removing her apron and her leather finger-thimbles. Nomore knew the loom was kept in the old scullery and yet when he was there, she was certain she heard the even tap of its under-oiled foot-treadle coming from upstairs.

No-more picked out the scarab, tracing the contours of its metallic thorax. From the direction of the house came the guttural pull of a car exhaust that set the magpies cawing out of the trees and Nomore, hard-rounding the yard, was just in time to see the back of Mr. Sylvain's car, chromed like the beetle she had pocketed, bounce out of the gate. She ran inside the house and up the stairs, calling for her mother who smiled at her from the vanity, pinning her hair with fresh grips, her skin a strange sheen like that of the frog she was keeping in her bedroom who seemed content enough to squat beneath the eaves which were damp and buzzed with bluebottles most days.

In her attic room, No-More took the rose-chafer from her jacket and set it on the bed. From beneath the mattress springs she pulled out a battered caddy in which she kept her other treasures: a photo of her mother, hair curled like a film star, the baby blanket she'd found amongst her father's affairs, the maths book she hadn't had the opportunity to return to school now that her mother needed her home. She ran her fingers over the numbers, how she missed their mystery, their voice. From downstairs, there was Mamie calling. *No more, No more.* She ran down the ladder to find her mother crumpled over the vanity, clothes strewn around her, the hairbrush, thimbles and the peacock feather, scattered, across the floor boards.

Is Mr Sylvain going to evict us? No-more said, returning the nib of the feather to its notch on the mirror's hinge. Her mother shook her head. 'So, there's nothing to cry about silly.' She stroked the tufts of her mother's shorn hair that had worked themselves loose from their grips.

'I found something beautiful today,' No-more said, longing to see her mother happy. She bolted back up the ladder only to find the beetle gone and the frog sat plump on its perch.

Bypass

Lifting the limp bodies of ortolans from yesterday's nets in a coppice so deep, Laurnadie can't hear anything but the rustle of leaves, can't hear the villagers start from their beds, unlatching shutters a thumb-width to watch the clutch of men in municipal overalls setting down their bait-boxes and flasks, recoiling from the pull-rope's tug on the generator, can't hear the sound of jack hammers, cement mixers, crockery rattling on every kitchen table, the swing of coffee bubbling at the pan edge. He can't see Mars slung horizon-low flickering off tools like a cold flame, the women cautious, leaving their front porches, swinging funnels they will force -feed the geese with, the men leading horse, plough share and coulter into fallow fields, shaking their hearts at the thought of *progress.*

No, in this sentry of trees, the old peasant cannot know that his world will soon be felled, drained, culverted, embanked, macadamed and tarred, so he warms his palms on his kindling fire, turning the skewer of bunting until small drops of fat make the cinders sizzle, pops each bird into his mouth, blithely crushing their tiny skulls.

It's a Man's World

The day they broke ground on the new road, Felix got hired as a banksman, greasing the points and repairing the ropes on the giant excavators that cut the batters and moved and flattened soil all day, everyday, around the clock. He was earning four times as much as he had been gutting swine and with his first pay packet, he settled the rent arrears due on the farm and bought back his father's mill pony from Old Rigal. When he walked it into the yard his mother wept and No-more dropped her darning and rushed up and hung off its bridle. She was happy it was home because more than anything, its smell was a reminder of her father and with her face buried in the old cob's mane she could almost believe he was still living.

Felix had told them all about the camp and the men that worked there - the fitters, steel-fixers, scaffolders, asphalt gangs and the machines that didn't need horses to pull them: the bladers, and scrapers, caterpillars and bulldozers. He unclipped a squat metal box with meshed perforations from his belt.

It was called a field radio and if a rope was broken and needed rethreading, the driver could call him on it day or night to come and fix it. 'Like plying yarn when spinning,' said No-more, who had done that a million times.

'Yes, just bigger,' said Felix, letting No-more press the radio to her ear. She heard a crackle like cherry wood burning and then a voice said 'Are you there, over?' She clapped her hands. 'I'm here, I'm here,' she cried, 'and I can thread anything with my eyes closed.'

'Give me that' said Felix leaning into the string of words. 'Roger' he said grabbing his gloves off the dresser. He patted No-more on the head. 'Don't be silly.' He unsnecked the latch of the front door. 'The motorway is no place for girls.' He stepped out into the dark yard leaving a trail of oil and silt behind him.

But No-more *had* seen girls at the camp, wheeling a copper boiler from a metal-clad lean-to, handing out galvanised cups of steaming tea and bread wrapped in greased paper to men resting on spade shafts or rolling cigarettes. She had seen them later too, as she returned from checking on Mamie's hives before dusk fell. They'd been tacking a scrap of velvet from the window lintel and lighting a flat-wick lantern behind it. Gathered in its red glow with their hands on their hips, hair held in flower grips, they sang roundels like lullabies but sadder - full of gazelles and pearl moons, the long road, the stars above it like tears, how the swallow never forgets the streams of home. From time to time a girl would drop out and a shadow would follow her into the shack, but the song would go on, round and round, over seas, through deserts and forests and well into the night.

No-more stabled the old cob and lit a candle in the outhouse to wash before bed. In front of the fratch of mirror nailed there, she pulled her hair back into a tight twist behind her ears and landed her hands on the bony outcrops of her hips. 'Over, Over,' she hummed at the light dancing off her cheekbones. 'Over, over,' her reflection sang back.

Hand Me Down

Smoking tight cheroots amongst the dolly tubs and poss sticks in the village washhouse, the women decided something had to be done about the Picard girl running around in her pinafore shifts and girlish culottes. Not that it was her fault her mother was maddled and paid her no mind and her father dead, but you couldn't call her a child anymore they nodded, exhaling tobacco smoke into the steam and lye, and with all the navvies coming to work the new road, they knew what might happen right enough.

They had watched them arrive, these men with leather skin and strange accents, hoiking toolboxes and steel-capped boots across their backs, setting up camp at the back of Rigal's twelve acre. At night the shanty silvered with the light of strung Tilley lamps and the thrum of guitars and laughter. The women stood at their fly screens watching Venus rise above the marsh mist while the flat irons heated on the grate. They asked their husbands why they didn't get road-work, they could make four times as much there as they did labouring old Sylvain's fields but the men just scratched their chins. *What did a farmer know of hoggin, concrete and tar? And once the thing was done, what then? Go back with their cap in their hands to Midas, who would most likely cut their wages and their wine allowance and raise their rent for the privilege. No, better to be safe and stay where they were.*

The women sighed, smoothing out the pleats on dresses they had worn when their waists didn't need to be corseted and their husbands had been young and brave. They took the irons off the fire and spat on them, feeling the crackle of heat evaporate to air.

The following morning, walking through Picard's farm with their hand-me-downs and a terrine of rillettes, they noted the broken handle on the water pump, the matt of brambles in the kaleyard. They rapped on the door, but the girl was already opening it, face lunar, hands running in circles.

They felt it then, ferrous and slick, a chill pull in their own bones. *What devil would do this, with the husband still cooling the earth?* They lifted the mother onto a chair in the fire nook, fetched the Pinard horn just to be sure, but they knew as they pressed their ear to the rise of skin, there would only be one heart there, keeping weary persistent time with itself.

After the curettage of Tansy and Pennyroyal had done the work the body was too weak to finish, and the small shape was swaddled in one of the dresses they had bought for the girl, they processed up the lane past where the houses and byres petered out, to where the soil was loam and giving. They were careful not to disturb the other mounds, some of them with wisps of decaying ribbon on them, a weathered bobbin, a pearl. The Picard girl, who looked so grown up in her borrowed clothes, bit off a glass button from the cuff of her dress and pushed it into the soft earth.

What devil? they thought, looking beyond the stretch of dark asphalt below and up into the canopy of poplars above, where when the sunlight touched the leaves, they glinted and rustled like gold coins.

The Mysteries of Bee Keeping Explained

...the first queen leaving her cell, enraged at the existence of others, makes it her business to destroy all rivals. To begin with she takes advantage of her younger competitors which are yet sealed up and of course cannot offer any resistance. She makes an opening to reach the abdomen and as soon as this is sufficiently large to admit her body, she thrusts it in, inflicting the fatal sting. If quick and spiteful movements are any indications of hatred, it is manifested here very plainly. The bees enlarge the orifice and drag out the dead queens. But if there is a plurality of queens in the hive then they sing to each other, a reedy piping. One will be shrill and fine, the other hoarse, short and quick. And then they will fight and when one queen remains the piping will cease, and no further trouble will be had.

Bid

Felix had his heart set on driving the machines. He was sick of being a banksman; all day the dirt and roil of clearing blades when they hit blue clay, or greasing ropes when they snapped. So, when the chargehand was asking if anyone knew of a place off-camp, to play cards and bring some girls, he said 'sure, I do', hoping the man would put a good word in for him with the foreman.

He cleaned up the disused drying shed that held nothing these days but a few wilted tobacco leaves hanging from the rafters and the old grain bin which would do as a table. His sister fished out a length of baize from Mamie's box of sewing scraps. 'There,' she said, laying it over the wood, smoothing out the corners. 'What time do we start?' Somewhere outside, they heard their mother's voice, shrill and fine, more a reedy piping than a song, but brother and sister smiled. It'd been sometime since they'd heard her singing.

'You can't play you know,' Felix said. Of course, he knew she *could* play, he knew she was a natural at reading cards, keeping tally of where the high values were, who had the low. He'd seldom beat her at Blackjack or Spades but this wasn't about the game he knew and it was certainly no place for little sisters. She didn't pout or burst into tears but stood glaring at him, with her hands on her waist and he realized how like their mother No-more had become, their mother before Da died, before her eyes took on that camsteery look of spooked cattle. Maybe it was the dress – he wondered where she'd got it and if she was wearing it specially for this – the way it fell about her hips, she seemed changed, grown up. 'You won't know the games,' he said upturning a water trough for a bench, 'but you can watch.'

The chargehand arrived with a fitter-mechanic known for stripping brass off engines and selling it on for scrap and a motor-scraper driver, who'd lost two fingers to a sprocket and chain accident. With them came three women; one of them Felix had been to see.

'Look who I brought along – your Sweet Pea' said the chargehand pouring four shots of Mirabelle schnapps from a flask. An anger flushed from Felix's groin. That's what he'd called her right enough, but it was their secret. They'd had plans, run away, set up somewhere south. *Slut*, he thought, *Bitch*.

They played Oh Hell, Crazy Eights and Mexican Sweat. The chargehand talked about hydraulics, the way the new machines dug soil like a knife through goose fat. Less work, more pay. He winked at No-more. Felix was giddy with the thought of it but also with the drink that roared through his head like the vibrations of a thirty-ton bulldozer. He hadn't wanted to win but he couldn't afford to lose this much. His sister had tried her best, an imperceptible nod or shake of the head, but his eyes had blurred with schnapps and he'd lost the count, so when the chargehand suggested one more hand, Felix replied as he'd heard at the pictures, 'too rich for my blood.'

'Don't worry,' said the chargehand, grabbing No-more by the hips and dropping her onto his lap, 'you can pay me when you are driving that Track Marshall 155.' Felix looked at his sister who stared back like the gilt pigs had done at the abattoir as he prodded them down the chutes. He looked down at his hand. 'Sure,' he said, his head revving with the sound of losing a heart but gaining a spade.

It will Hurt Less

…if you remember it like this: Mamie singing to bees, your shadow stretched, substantial as the hayloft, the horse turning in the wheelhouse, its bald muzzle puckering for hay. The man. His mouth – the bristle of unharvested corn, the chafe of cattle at the trough. Your arms a frenzy of wings.

Remember how the sun slipped red off the horizon, how you held its glow for a second in the palm of your hand. How it crested the rim of your eyes. Then it was gone, the sky a silvery backdrop of blue and that's when you counted the moon, you counted the moon.

Progress

Larnaudie was squatted on the canal bank, sautéing mushrooms in a knob of goose fat, when he heard something crashing about in the forest's undergrowth. At first he thought it was boar that like him, were foraging for the Chanterelles and Penny Buns that clustered fresh and dewy under the chestnut trees or the caiman they'd said had escaped the zoo in the floods; but when he heard cursing he figured it was probably one of the surveyors working on the new road, come to stick steel pins tied with orange ribbons all about the place, the ones Larnuadie always removed and used to skewer bunting with. *The forest will be a coppice soon*, he thought, taking the skillet off the heat.

When he heard crying, he stood up; a young man, torso bent over the old well was hitting his head with his fists. *So it was Felix Picard that hid Madame Bazin's rifle*, Larnaudie thought. He had found it lodged there a few years back while gathering maidenhair fern for a sore throat. The rubber had rotted, and the firing pin snapped, but he'd repaired it and used it to scare stoats out of stealing his chicks and eggs. *I was the same when my mother died, sure enough. Mad-cat at everything and everyone.* He thought about his brother also, hung for stealing money which he hadn't, Larnaudie knew, because he'd been there too, in this very wood, staking rabbit snares, when the allied plane swooped low and the clutch of white parachutes fluttered into the clearing close to where he was setting his traps. He'd dropped the noose he was tying and sat low, watched a shadow gather up the parachutes and their gummed packages and disappear again into the clutter of scrub. It wasn't his brother that he was sure of because he'd been with his pal Florian Picard, hung as well later that day, but he had no proof and his testament would have been seen as sooted anyway.

Soon after, that young lizard Sylvain had offered to buy the land that the grieving families had no way to work without their men-folk and Larnaudie had always wondered how the bastard son of a widow, who kept a café and took in washing, could afford to buy 1000 ares of good farming land and pay others to tend it. In his heart though, he'd always known and he realized now, looking at young Felix lashed with rage, that it was the reason he'd hidden himself for a life-time in this place of roots, half-light and marsh mist.

Larnaudie went over to Felix Picard and offered him a fat slither of mushroom. 'Sorry for your trouble lad,' he said, sitting down beside him on the mossy rounds of stone. Pigeons cooed in the branches; nutria rustled under leaf litter. Then there was something else, a low hum underscored by footfall and they both looked to where the river looped back on itself. Old Sylvain was thrashing, hands flailing above his head, through the thickets of butterbur that lined the stream, behind him, a lattice of bees. They watched as Sylvain plunged into the water and the swarm dipped then rose up into the tree canopy and disappeared. Sylvain surfaced and Felix rushed to his feet but Larnaudie put a hand across his chest. 'Steady on lad,' he said, flicking his knife open, scraping its blade under his fingernails. And although both witnessed it, they'd never be quite sure if it really happened; two slit pupils rose from the water's surface, a pair of scaled nostrils flared and a set of bony jaws snapped down on Sylvain and he was gone.

'Is this what you were looking for,' said Larnaudie to Felix, pulling out the rifle from the knot of a wych-elm. Felix shook his head, got up and took the deer path toward the new road.

Progress indeed, thought Larnaudie.

Last Word

After the funeral, No-more went to the coppice and cut down the skeps her mother had hung there. She sat in the yard unravelling each one until they returned to what they had been to start with: fat skeins of bailing twine. The land and air lay quiet about her. The motorway gangs had gone south to open up a new piece of road and Felix had left with them, a driver now, not just a banksman. Rigal's twelve acre, where the camp had been, was a field again, with only a few sheets of metal and scraps of velvet testament to what had been there before. No-more stacked the twine then went inside to sort through her mother's things with a quiet hope she might find a note to explain why she had done what she had done. She pulled out a small suitcase from the tallboy and in it placed her mother's Sunday dress, the peacock feather that had always hung from the vanity stand, the least worn of the frocks the village women had given her and the book on trigonometry she had kept under her bed and never returned to the school. A photograph fell out of it, one she had never seen before. On the left was Papie with his curled moustache, staring straight at the camera. The girl strapped to him with horse leathers was her of course – she remembered his heartbeat, the smell of his sweat. Then there was Felix, a toddler in a sailor suit, eyes a tantrum. Next to him were six other boys in varying stages of manhood: the brothers who had left home before she knew them. At the end of the line stood her mother, eyes looking over the camera and out into the distance. The farm was a misty outline behind them. She turned the picture over; a faded looped script, her mother's, covered the back:

Maurice, Katrine, Constantine, Tristan, Florian, Miguel, Fabian, Renaud, Felix

Below this, in fresh ink her mother's hand again, shaky and faint, a name – Arielle.

She said it over and over again, her mother's last word not voiced but written, listening to the syllables soft pressure pleat her palate: Ar-i-elle, Ar-i-elle, Ar-i-elle. She slipped the photograph back between the pages of her maths book and into the suitcase. Then, she sat at the vanity and twisted her hair into a high plait and with the scissors she used to chop the skeps down, she cut her hair. It fell in blunt lines around her ears and it felt as light as empty honeycomb.

She stepped on to the bus with her small suitcase just as someone with the same heft and look to him as her father stepped off. Constantine? Tristan? Florian? Miguel? Fabian? Renaud? She smiled in the knowledge that wishes did come true but not necessarily when you need them.

The bus followed the canal past the alder trees, the drying kilns, the angelica fields, past the school and the big house where Sylvain, who had been missing for days, lived, past Hangman's Lane where the traitors and miscarried were buried, past the church where her father had fallen to his death. Then they were out on to the new road, its white-lines crisp, its metal barriers a curve of zinc. She hummed the name as the bus idled over the hill, at which point she looked back at the village. All she saw was the chamfered gleam of the weathervane as the sun went down.

She rolled the name around her head in time to the bus's rattle and sway, but as much as she repeated the word, she could find no part of herself within it, nothing that belonged to who she was except perhaps the memory of catching damselflies some hazy autumn day a long time ago or her mother offering her a wand of bee-bread. No, she thought No-more will do.

Acknowledgements

Scarab was first published in Barren Magazine in 2020, *A Girl's Guide to Frog Gigging* in The Cabinet of Heed in 2019. *No-more* was published in Mslexia Magazine entitled *Mathematics for Girls* in 2018, *Weathervane* was published in Flash Fiction Magazine in 2017 and Reflex Fiction published *Postpartum* in 2017.

The Mysteries Of Bee-Keeping Explained is an extract from *Mysteries Of Bee-Keeping Explained: Being A Complete Analysis Of The Whole Subject; Consisting Of The Natural History Of Bees, Directions For Obtaining The Greatest Amount Of Pure Surplus Honey With The Least Possible Expense, Remedies For Losses Given, And The Science Of "Luck" Fully Illustrated—The Result Of More Than Twenty Years' Experience In Extensive Apiaries* by M. Quinby, Practical Bee-Keeper. New York: C. M. Saxton, Agricultural Book Publisher, 152 Fulton Street. 1853.

About the Author

Mary-Jane is passionate about writing, teaching and editing creative writing. A Forward Prize nominee and Hawthornden fellow, Mary-Jane has won the Live Canon Pamphlet Prize, the Bridport Poetry prize, Martin Starkie, Dromineer, Reflex Fiction and Mslexia Flash prize as well as the Bedford Poetry competition. In 2020, she was shortlisted for the Beverley International Prize for Literature and longlisted for the UK National Poetry Prize. Other publications include *Heliotrope with Matches and Magnifying Glass* ipublished by Pindrop Press and *Dihedral* by Live Canon

Her work appears in anthologies including *Best Small Fictions 2014/16/18* and *Best Microfictions 2020* and in a variety of publications including *Magma, Modern Poetry in Translation, The Journal of Compressed Creative Arts, Tishman Review, Magma, Barren, Spelk, Cabinet of Heed, Firewords, Flashback Fiction, Mslexia, Fictive Dream, The Lonely Crowd*, and *Prole.*

She has an MA (Distinction) in Creative Writing from Kellogg College, Oxford and is currently studying for a PhD in poetry and translation at Newcastle University.

Mary-Jane teaches courses and workshops on short fiction, microfiction, memoir, poetry and the novel.